THE CASE OF THE
INCAPACITATED

by **Robin Pulver**

illustrated by **Lynn Rowe Reed**

Holiday House / New York

Library of Congress Cataloging-in-Publication Data
Pulver, Robin.
The case of the incapacitated capitals / by Robin Pulver ;
illustrated by Lynn Rowe Reed. — 1st ed.
p. cm.
Summary: Capital letters are being so neglected in
Mr. Wright's classroom that they are nearly
incapacitated, and a medical team must be summoned
to perform CPR— Capital Posture Repair.
ISBN 978-0-8234-2402-3 (hardcover)
[1. Alphabet—Fiction. 2. Teachers—Fiction.
3. Schools—Fiction.] I. Reed, Lynn Rowe, ill. II. Title.
PZ7.P97325Cas 2012   [E]—dc23   2011024047

*With appreciation for
hardworking, dedicated
teachers everywhere!
And for Weenie Scoop,
Yard, and Buttercup.
(You know who you are.)*
—R. P. (aka Ninsk)

**To Tyler Johnson
—L. R. R.**

It was the first Tuesday in May, a beautiful spring day. But in Mr. Wright's classroom, the capital letters were in sad shape.

What's the matter with you?
The small letters worried.
Why aren't you doing your jobs?

The capital letters whimpered and moaned.

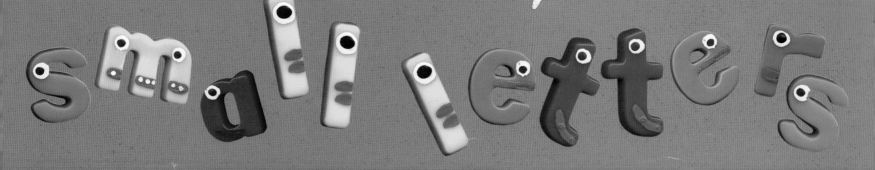

We want to take the lead in spelling out proper names of people, places, and things . . .

. . . and days of the week . . . special days and holidays . . . and months of the year.

Normally it's our pleasure to make sure sentences get off to a good start.

And we're always happy to band together if a word needs special attention, such as **EXIT** or **STOP** or **DANGER!**

We take our tasks seriously . . .

. . . but lately the kids have forgotten about us and now we're . . .

. . . out of oomph!
Zapped!
Goners!
Incapacitated!
First Aid
WATERPROOF TAPE

Meanwhile, for **M**r. **W**right's students, school began as usual. **B**ut as morning moved toward noon, **M**r. **W**right looked more and more miserable.

Mr. Wright looks as bad as our uppercase friends!

"**M**r. **W**right, what's wrong?" asked **S**am.

Mr. **W**right sighed. "**D**o you realize what day this is?"

"It's Tuesday!" said Cate.
"What else?" asked Mr. Wright.
"Pizza Day in the cafeteria!" said Ting.
Mr. Wright groaned. "You forgot
Teacher Appreciation Day.
It's always the first Tuesday in May."

Let me remind you, if I may, that without me May wouldn't be a month.

The kids felt bad. They decided to write a letter to the principal, Ms. Allcap.
"Don't peek, Mr. Wright!" said Bud. "It's a surprise."

When the kids were finished, they showed **M**r. **W**right what they'd written. "**T**his should cheer you up."

may 4

ms. allcap, principal
learnalot elementary school
37 forget-me-not lane
capital city, wisconsin 53305

dear ms. allcap:
it's teacher appreciation day! we think you should give mr. wright this friday off from school to show how much we appreciate him.

sincerely,
mr. wright's class

Horrors! **N**othing in this letter is capitalized as it should be.

The principal will be appalled!

How embarrassing!

If only we had the strength to fix it.

"**W**e'll call for help! **B**ut who should we say needs assistance? **C**apital letters? **O**r uppercase letters?" asked the small letters. "**I**t doesn't matter! **T**hey're the same thing!" said the capitals.

The small letters sent out an **SOS**:

Save Our Sentences! Capital letters-aka upper-case incapacitated!

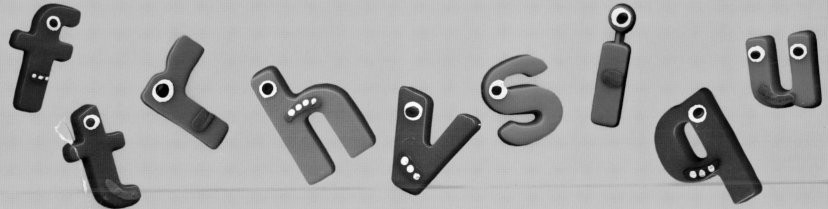

Mr. Wright smiled wanly. "I appreciate the thought," he said, "but writing a letter is not the same as texting. You've forgotten something important."

The kids looked around. "Oops! We forgot to water the plants!"

"I'm talking about your letter," said Mr. Wright. "For instance, my name. What's wrong with it?"

The kids were stumped. "Nothing, Mr. Wright," said Carlos. "Your name fits you because you're usually right."

"Is 'Usually' your first name?" asked Cate.

Bud said, "If it is, you probably wish you had a nickname, like me."

"My name is *not* 'Usually,'" said Mr. Wright, "and I don't need a nickname. My mother already gave me one when I was little. The initials are C. B., but that's all I'm telling."

Now the kids were dying to know.
"Cry Baby?" asked Sam.
"Cutie Boy?" guessed Ting.

"**R**ight," said **M**r. **W**right. "**N**ow what about the sentences in this letter? **H**ow should they begin?"

"**T**he first one starts with *i*," said **C**ate, "and the other starts with *w*. **W**e got *that* right!"

"**G**rrrrrr!" growled **M**r. **W**right. "**T**he first letter of a sentence should be capitalized! **Y**ou also need to capitalize the day, month, school, street, city, and state. **A**nd don't forget to capitalize **T**eacher **A**ppreciation **D**ay because it's a holiday."

"**A** holiday?" gasped the kids. "**H**ow come we have school? **W**e could appreciate you even more from home!"

"**T**his is not a day-off-from-school holiday," said **M**r. **W**right. "**I**t's a special day like **V**alentine's **D**ay . . . or **P**ajama **D**ay . . . or **D**rop **E**verything and **R**ead **D**ay."

Or **N**ational **P**unctuation **D**ay!

Remember when the cafeteria served meat loaf shaped like us?

"**A**re we supposed to wear teacher clothes today? **O**r drop everything and appreciate you?" asked **R**ose.

"**Y**ou're supposed to be extra nice to me," said **M**r. **W**right.

"**Y**ou can start by capitalizing my name."

That's when the kids discovered that the uppercase letters were in an alarming condition.

I'm failing fast!

I'm collapsing!

Z-Z-Z-Z-Z-Z

I seem to be sagging.
I can't jump at all!
THE RESCUERS SHOULD BE HERE BY NOW!

When the kids tried to capitalize, the uppercase letters stumbled and staggered into all the wrong places.

An emergency team careened into the classroom. The medics quickly diagnosed the problem. "It's a case of serious neglect!"

WHRRRRRR

EMERGENCY

Phew!

First Aid
WATERPROOF TAPE

IV

Some uppercase letters needed **CPPR** (**C**apital **P**osition and **P**osture **R**epair). **M**any required extra support. **T**he medics injected them all with fresh, fortified ink.

Much better!
Thank you!

"**L**isten up, kids," said a medic. "**Y**ou know how muscles get flabby when you don't exercise? **S**ame for uppercase letters. **U**se 'em or lose 'em."

Later, with uppercase assistance, the kids revised their letter to the principal. "Mr. Wright," said Bud, "if we capitalized perfectly, will you *please* tell us your nickname?"

"Okay," said Mr. Wright. "But I bet I won't have to."

May 4

Ms. Allcap, Principal
Learnalot Elementary School
37 Forget-Me-Not Lane
Capital City, Wisconsin 53305

Dear Ms. Allcap:
  It's Teacher Appreciation Day! We think you should give Mr. Wright this Friday off from school to show how much we appreciate him.

Sincerely,
Mr. Wright's Class

P.S. We could take Friday off too. Then you won't have to get a substitute.

Mr. Wright studied the letter, searching for a mistake. But the kids got it all right.

Even the greeting and the closing!

"You win." He gulped. "My mother called me . . . um . . . Mom still calls me Cuddly Bunny."

Finally the kids stopped laughing.

"Mr. Wright," said Bud, "we appreciate you *so* much, tomorrow has to be Give Your Teacher a Better Nickname Day!"

The End

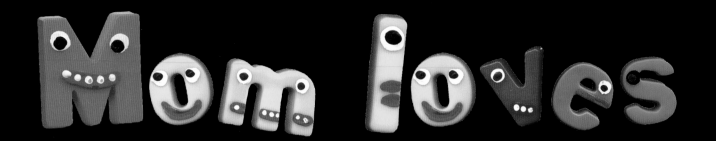

How **CAPITAL LETTERS** got their other name

Capital letters haven't always been known as uppercase. In the days before computers and even typewriters, books and newspapers and magazines were printed using hand-operated machines called printing presses.

Back then, every single capital letter and every small letter (also known as minuscule letter) was carved on its own little wood block. The printer set each letter of every word and sentence into long narrow trays. Then he rolled ink over the letters and printed them onto paper.

All the letters were stored in large open cases. Capital letters and small letters were kept in separate cases so they wouldn't get mixed up and so the printer could quickly find the letter he needed.

And guess what? The case of capital letters was always above the case of small letters, so the printers called the capital letters "uppercase" and small letters "lowercase"!

What to capitalize in a letter

January 15, 2037 ← *the months of the year*

Mr. Wright ← *titles and proper names*
Mile High Elementary School ← *the names of schools*
47 Rocket Road ← *streets*
Capital City, Wisconsin 53305 ← *cities and towns, states*

Dear Mr. Wright, ← *the greeting, title, and
proper names*

   We were surprised to learn that your father ← *the first letter of each sentence*
was a teacher at the old Learnalot Elementary ← *the names of buildings*
School when my mother was in school. That school
was not as much fun as this one. It was on the ground
instead of a mile up into space. Instead of riding the
yellow heli-rocket to school, the students rode on a
yellow bus that went really slow. Did you know that
Teacher Appreciation Day is next month? It is the ← *holidays*
first Tuesday in May. My mother reminded me! ← *days of the week / months*

Sincerely, ← *closing*
Poindexter ← *proper names*

Some useful rules about when to use capital letters

- Always capitalize the first word of a sentence.

  Would you like to go to school in a heli-rocket?

- The pronoun "I" is always capitalized.

  The last time I forgot my homework I was embarrassed.

- The days of the week and the months of the year and holidays are capitalized.

  The fourth Thursday of every November is Thanksgiving Day.

- Capitalize the names of individual people.

  Mr. Wright's class wished that they could have

  met George Washington Carver in person.

- When titles come before a proper name, they are capitalized.

  Mr. Wright and Ms. Allcap are on their way to meet Senator Winner.

- Capitalize the names of cities, towns, states, and countries.

  The students live either in Capital City or in the nearby towns of Rushmore

  and Morton, which are all in Wisconsin in the United States of America.

- The names of nationalities and languages are capitalized.

  Most Australians speak English.

- Capitalize the names of groups of people and organizations.

  The Parent Teacher Association has lots of Democrats, Republicans,

  and Independents in it.

- Specific places such as schools or buildings or structures with names are capitalized.

  The Mountain Middle School is located near the Capital Bridge.

- Geographic features such as oceans, mountains, rivers, and lakes.

  You can see the Pacific Ocean from the top of some of the Cascade Mountains.